WOULD YOU CLIMB A BANANA?

Library of Congress Cataloging-in-Publication Data
Woodworth, Viki
Would You Climb a Banana? / Viki Woodworth
p. cm.
Summary: A rhyming verse describes the joys of exercise.
ISBN 1-56766-074-6
1. Exercise for children-juvenile literature.
[1. Exercise.]
I. Title
GV481.W66 1994   92-40672
613.7'042-dc20   CIP/AC

WOULD YOU CLIMB A BANANA?

by Viki Woodworth

THE CHILD'S WORLD

Viki Woodworth and family.

What could you climb on a warm afternoon?

A banana?

A tree?

A fox

or a moon?

(A tree)

A lady bug?
A loon?

**A pool
or a rose?**

(A pool)

What's fun to jump almost anytime?

A rope?
Macaroni?

A rhino
or a lime?

(A rope)

A hill

or a bow?

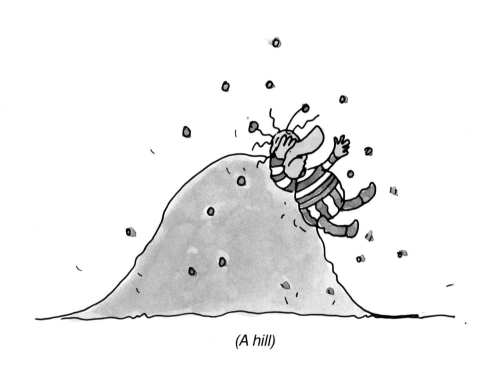

(A hill)

Whatever the season,
in any weather,

plenty of exercise

will make
you feel better!